THANK YOU TO...

All of the Virginia Beach Goldendoodles for loving your owners
every day and enhancing lives everywhere you go!

Mom, Dad, Mark, Jack, Connor, & Austin
for encouragement, support, & love.

Shenleigh O'Doodle for being the **BEST DOG EVER**
and for 14 years of companionship & adventure!

Library of Congress Control Number: 2021905882
ISBN: 978-1-7362567-2-5 (Hardback)
      978-1-7362567-3-2 (Paperback)
      978-1-7362567-4-9 (ebook)

Illustrations by Harry Aveira
Cover Design by Praise Saflor
Format and Layout by Glaiza Beverly Ganaba

Published in the United States of America

SHENLEIGH
O'DOODLE
Half Golden, Half Poodle

By Annesley M. Hackathorn   Illustrated by Harry Aveira

"Today will be my **BEST DAY EVER!**" shouts Shenleigh O'Doodle! "I'm going to Happy Paws Daycare!"

"Look at that cute Springer Spaniel pup," Shenleigh says, as she enters the busy play yard. "She looks **JUST** like her parents! And that Doberman Pinscher pup looks just like **HIS** parents!"

HAPPY PAWS DAY CARE

Shenleigh looks down at her own curly blonde hair. Then she looks up at her mom and dad. "I don't look like either one of you," she says.

Mom smiles. "That's because you're a mix of two different dog breeds. Dad is a Golden Retriever and I'm a Standard Poodle."

"Does that make me a misfit? Will the other puppies still like me?" Shenleigh asks sadly.

"Oh, Shenleigh," answers Mom.
"That makes you unique. You are a beautiful Goldendoodle. You are Shenleigh O' Doodle,
half Golden, half Poodle!"

A small brown and white dog with long floppy ears runs up to Shenleigh. His legs are so short that his tummy almost touches the ground.

"Hi! I'm Fred and I'm a mixed breed too. My mom is a Fox Terrier and my dad is a Bassett Hound."

"Cool!" says Shenleigh. "Between us, I'll bet there's a lot we can do."

The Springer Spaniel pup walks by,
along with a big Doberman Pinscher.
After a quick sniff, the Doberman snorts,
"My name is Danny. Why are you so curly?"

"I'm **UNIQUE**,"
Shenleigh answers proudly.

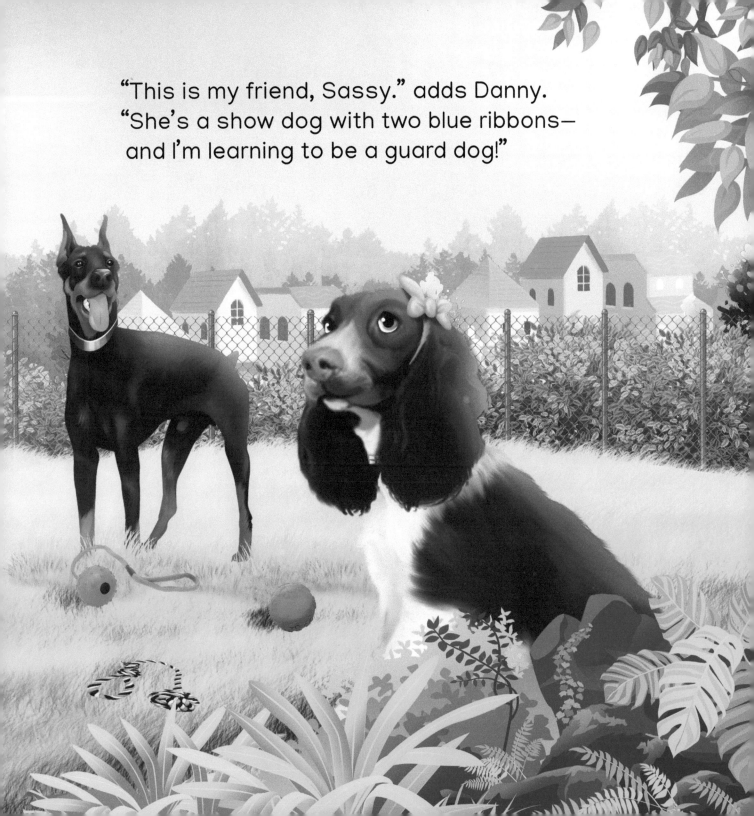

"This is my friend, Sassy." adds Danny.
"She's a show dog with two blue ribbons—
and I'm learning to be a guard dog!"

"What can **YOU** do?" asks Sassy, looking very pleased with herself.

Shenleigh calmly answers, "I plan to be a service dog so I can help people, but I can do lots of things."

"Me too," says Fred, as Danny and Sassy shrug and walk away. Shenleigh meets many new friends— like Barney the Boxer and Chi Chi the Chihuahua. But she's sure her very **BEST** friend is Fred.

The next day, when Shenleigh and Fred go outside to play, they notice something strange.
The play yard is empty!

"Look! There's a big hole in the fence," yells Shenleigh.
"This is terrible!"

"**OH NO!** Everyone is gone," Fred squeals.
"The puppies got out! How will we ever find them?"

Fred has an idea. "Shenleigh, since your dad is a Golden Retriever, I'll bet you have a great sense of smell. And since your mom is a Standard Poodle, you must be really smart."

"Yes!" says Shenleigh. "And your mom is a Fox Terrier, so I'll bet you can walk a long, long way— even though your legs are short. And with your dad being a Basset Hound, you must know how to search!"

"We make a **PERFECT TEAM**," says Shenleigh. "Together we will find our missing playmates."

Shenleigh sniffs the ground.
"I smell the scent of the puppies...
I smell tires...
and I smell hay!"

She puts her nose to the
ground and follows the scent.
Fred also picks up the scent
and runs beside her, going as
fast as his little legs will go.

Shenleigh keeps thinking, "Puppies? Tires? Hay?"
"I know!" he suddenly shouts.
"We must search for the puppies
in a truck filled with hay!"

"Yes!" says Fred.

She keeps her nose to the ground,
but suddenly realizes that Fred has disappeared.

"Fred, where are you?" she calls out.

"Yip! Yip! Over here!" squeals Fred.

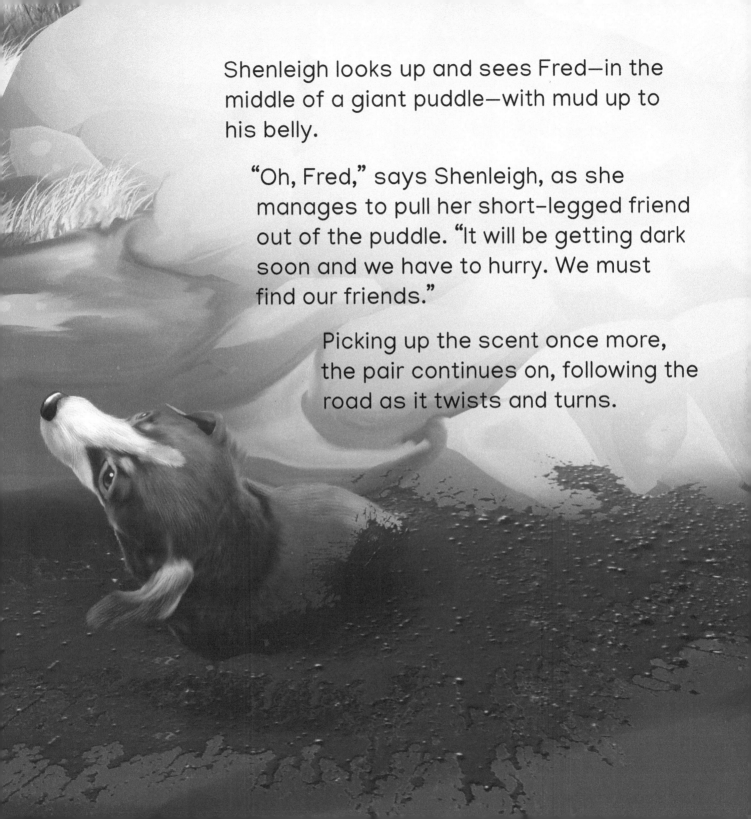

Shenleigh looks up and sees Fred—in the middle of a giant puddle—with mud up to his belly.

"Oh, Fred," says Shenleigh, as she manages to pull her short-legged friend out of the puddle. "It will be getting dark soon and we have to hurry. We must find our friends."

Picking up the scent once more, the pair continues on, following the road as it twists and turns.

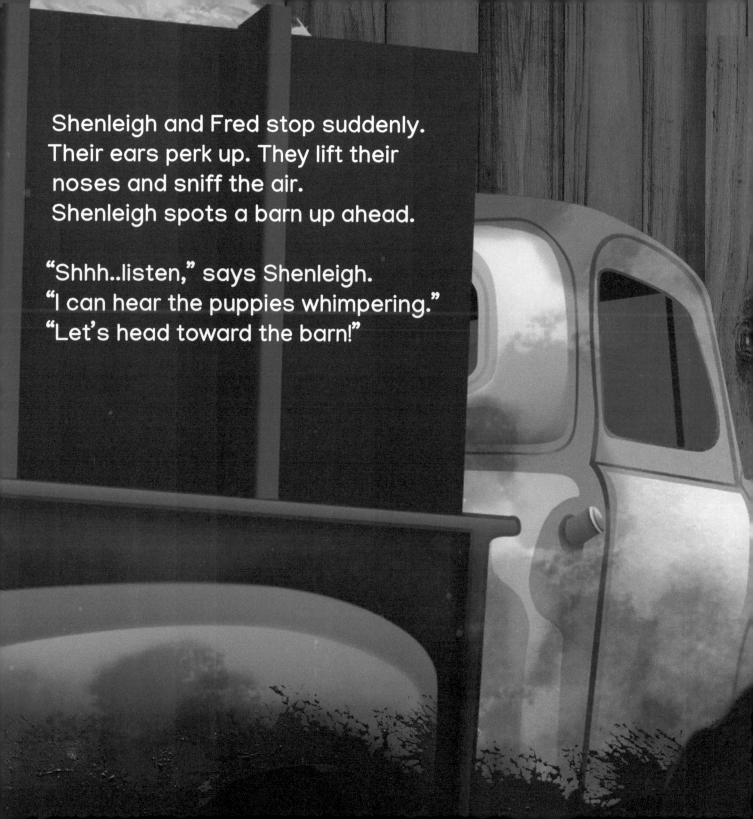

Shenleigh and Fred stop suddenly.
Their ears perk up. They lift their
noses and sniff the air.
Shenleigh spots a barn up ahead.

"Shhh..listen," says Shenleigh.
"I can hear the puppies whimpering."
"Let's head toward the barn!"

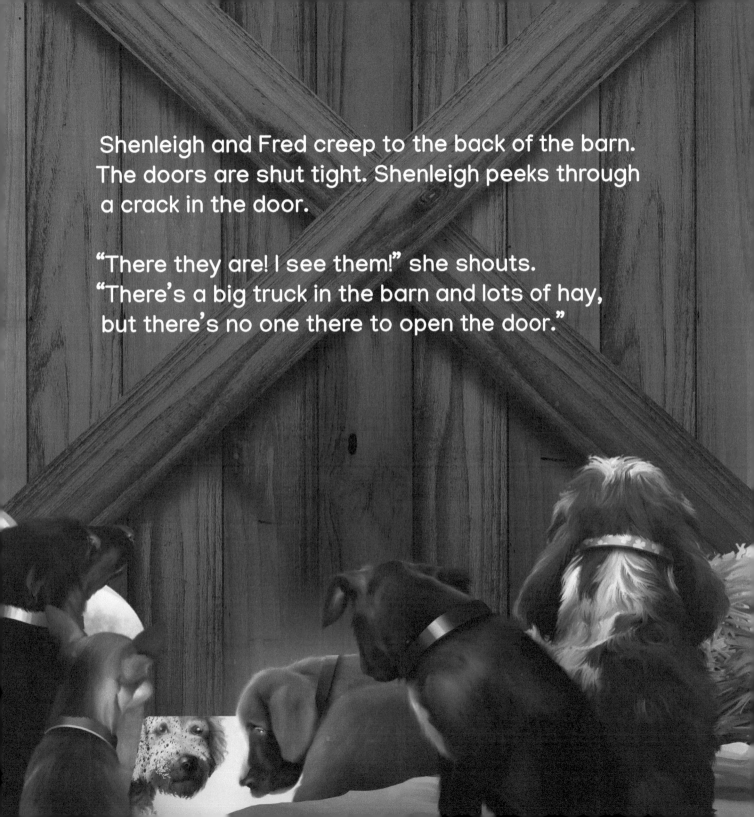

Shenleigh and Fred creep to the back of the barn.
The doors are shut tight. Shenleigh peeks through
a crack in the door.

"There they are! I see them!" she shouts.
"There's a big truck in the barn and lots of hay,
but there's no one there to open the door."

"I think I can help," Fred says, poking his nose through a tiny hole under the barn door. "I can make this hole big enough for all the puppies to escape."

Then, with his small—but strong—Fox Terrier legs, Fred starts to dig. Shenleigh crouches beside him.

Soon, one final push with those short, powerful legs and Fred is inside the barn! He grabs Shenleigh's collar and helps her through the hole.

"WE'RE HERE TO GET YOU OUT!"
announces Shenleigh. The puppies squeal with delight.

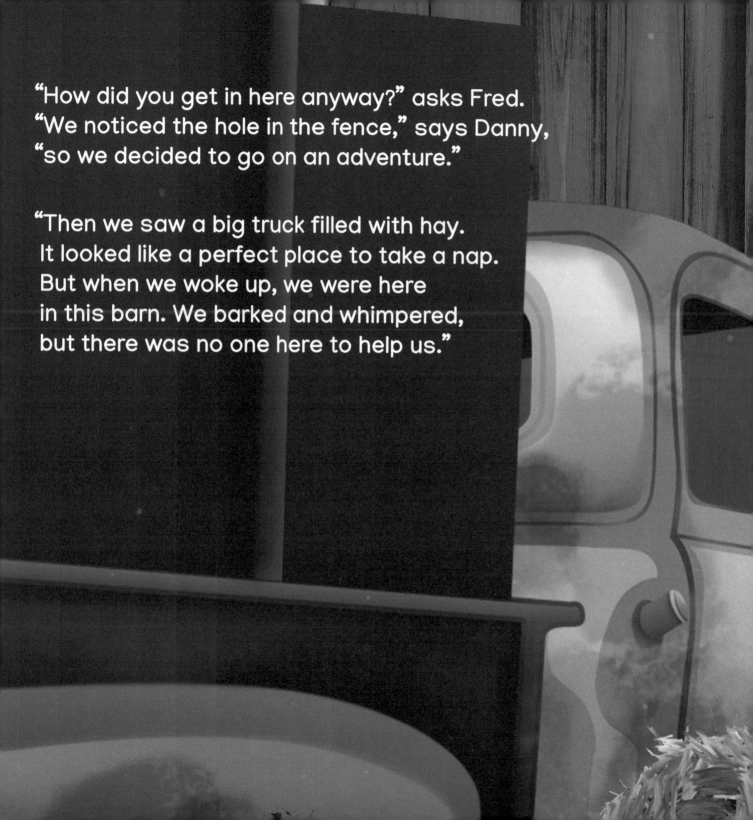

"How did you get in here anyway?" asks Fred.
"We noticed the hole in the fence," says Danny,
"so we decided to go on an adventure."

"Then we saw a big truck filled with hay.
It looked like a perfect place to take a nap.
But when we woke up, we were here
in this barn. We barked and whimpered,
but there was no one here to help us."

"We're tired and hungry," says Sassy.
"Can you help us get back to the daycare?"

"We will get you out," Shenleigh says,
"but we have to hurry. It will soon be dark."

One by one, the puppies scramble under the
door and rush out into the cool evening air.

Shenleigh takes charge.

"Okay pups, stay together and follow me. My nose will get us back home. Fred, you follow behind so no one gets lost. And stay out of mud puddles!"

Shenleigh knows the puppies are counting on her. She must get everyone back safely. She leads the way as they troop down the road, following the twists and turns.

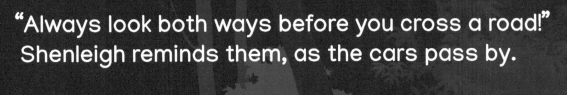

"Always look both ways before you cross a road!"
Shenleigh reminds them, as the cars pass by.

"Mud puddle up ahead!" warns Fred.
All of the puppies walk carefully around the puddle.

"WE'RE ALMOST THERE!" shouts Shenleigh.

Finally, they see the bright lights of the daycare. The happy, yelping puppies run to their parents. The pups are hugged and kissed—then scolded for running off. Fred's mom is busy cleaning mud off her little guy.

The puppies shout, **"SHENLEIGH AND FRED ARE OUR HEROES!"**

"How did you find them?" asks Danny's dad.

Fred smiles. "We used the talents we were born with.
Shenleigh is a Goldendoodle! She's very smart and
has a great sense of smell."

Shenleigh smiles. "And if Fred didn't search like
a Basset Hound and dig like a Fox Terrier,
we wouldn't have gotten into the barn
in the first place!"

Danny and Sassy jump up
to get everyone's attention.

"We have something to say,"
says Danny, raising his voice.

"We're sorry that we were not always nice to the brave puppies who brought us home safely. We are so proud of Fred, our muddy little terrier...

and SHENLEIGH O'DOODLE, HALF GOLDEN, HALF POODLE!"

DID YOU ENJOY THE BOOK?

It would mean so much if you could leave us a review on Amazon.com or Goodreads.

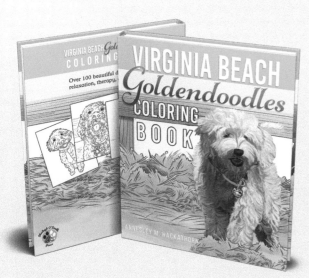

Check out this other great title from Annesley M. Hackathorn.

Visit virginiabeachgoldendoodles.com and grab free coloring pages.

ABOUT THE AUTHOR

Annesley Magill Hackathorn, born in Ireland to spectacular supportive parents, grew up in Pittsburgh, PA and now lives in beautiful Virginia Beach, VA.

Annesley's career as an elementary guidance counselor enabled her to empower many students, guiding them to find confidence and strength in their differences. She believes we all should use our uniqueness and diversity to accomplish incredible things and follow our dreams. We all have special talents!

An avid dog lover, Annesley has owned, loved, rescued and trained a multitude of dogs. She became fascinated with the Goldendoodle, a unique blend of Standard Poodle and Golden Retriever. Shenleigh O'Doodle, her BEST DOG EVER, was born in 2003, the first puppy from Virginia Beach Goldendoodles, where Annesley continues to breed these top-quality dogs.

ABOUT THE ILLUSTRATOR

Harry Aveira has been creating children's books for 20 years with more than a hundred books (and counting). He loves partnering with authors to help bring their stories to life. Harry lives in Indonesia with his two daughters and his wife.

GOLDENDOODLES

- Are a cross of 2 breeds of dogs so they are considered to be a hybrid, a mix of a Golden Retriever and a Poodle

- Can be different sizes: standard, mini, and toy

- Can be many different colors: white, cream, brown, gold, red, silver, and black. They can also have some different patterns such as parti (2 colors)

- Can have many desirable traits : intelligent, loyal, friendly, easy going, trainable, and energetic

- Can be trained to be therapy dogs to help people. A therapy dog gives comfort and support to people in hospitals, schools, retirement homes, disasters, etc. by helping people to feel better

- Can also be trained to be service dogs. A **service dog** has special training and helps a person who needs help with an everyday activity such as walking, hearing, or seeing. These dogs can be trained to open doors, pull wheelchairs, retrieve dropped items, bring someone their phone, and many other tasks to help their owner live a better life. Goldendoodles can also provide emotional and behavioral support to people with autism, depression, or anxiety. They can be taught to detect seizures and even alert diabetics to high and low sugar levels! Service dogs have special training so they can go everywhere with their person!

- Make great family pets

- LOVE people

CPSIA information can be obtained
at www.ICGtesting.com
Printed in the USA
BVHW022205230421
605781BV00006B/30

9 781736 256725